"**CARNIVOROUS**, ADJ.: ADDICTED TO THE CRUELTY OF DEVOURING THE TIMOROUS VEGETARIAN, HIS HEIRS AND ASSIGNS".

AMBROSE BIERCE
"THE DEVIL'S DICTIONARY", 1906

RUUUUUMBLE!
TENS OF MILES SOUTH OF THE **TEMPLE MOUND CITY OF CAHOKIA** (PRESENT DAY ILLINOIS), APRIL, 1564
A SMALL ARMY OF *CONQUISTADORS* ADVANCES SLOWLY, WEAKENED BY A THREE MONTHS JOURNEY UNDER THE UNFORGIVING WEATHER OF THE **GREAT PLAINS**...
LURED BY HIS GENERAL WITH THE PROMISE OF A GREAT TREASURE RUMORED TO BE BURIED AT **CAHOKIA**, THEY ARE GROWING IMPATIENT AND EMBITTERED...

GENERAL **PEDRO DE SOTO**, KNOWN TO HIS MEN SIMPLY AS **"DON PEDRO"**, IS THE LEADER OF THIS SMALL ARMY OF GOLD-SEEKING *CONQUISTADORS* TRAVELING ACROSS THESE UNTAMED TERRITORIES...
DON PEDRO'S MOST TRUSTED OFFICERS ARE CAPTAIN **GONZALO JIMENEZ DE LEON**, KNOWN TO HIS COMRADES AS **"EL RUBIO"**...
...AND LIEUTENANT **VASCO NUMEZ DE BALBOA**, BETTER KNOWN AS **"EL LADINO"**.

A YOUNG CHOCTAW INDIAN CALLED **TECUMSEH** RELUCTANTLY GUIDES THEM TO THE TEMPLE MOUND CITY OF CAHOKIA, UNDER THE THREAT OF DON PEDRO AND HIS OFFICERS RAPING AND KILLING HIS BELOVED WIFE, **ITZEL**...
POR TODOS LOS DIABLOS, **LADINO**. AREN'T YOU THIRSTY?
NEVER, *COMPRENDE?*

TELL ME, YOUNG **TECUMSEH**, AND DO NOT LIE TO ME AS YOU'VE DONE BEFORE: **HOW MUCH LONGER TILL WE REACH CAHOKIA?**
IT IS FOOLISH TO FOLLOW THE TRAIL OF **IKTOMI**. HE KNOWS NOTHING BUT TRICKS AND HE WILL BRING NOTHING BUT TROUBLE FOR ALL OF US!
DON PEDRO DID NOT ASK FOR YOUR COUNSEL, SLAVE!
HOW MUCH LONGER, SLAVE?
WE WILL REACH CAHOKIA TOMORROW AFTERNOON, MASTER.
BY SUNDOWN TOMORROW, *JEFE*, WE SHALL ALL BATHE IN GOLD!

XIBALBA, BETTER KNOWN AS "THE PLACE WHERE THE SUN REFUSES TO SHINE"...
THE WASICHU WILL ARRIVE TOMORROW, LORD HURACAN.
HURACAN SHALL RULE OVER THE UPPER WORLD THE SAME WAY HE DID 400 WINTERS AGO...
THROUGH BLOOD!
BE QUIET, UXAH! HURACAN HAS NOT ASKED FOR YOUR COUNSEL, SO WHY SHOULD HE ATTACH IMPORTANCE TO YOUR SILLY SUPERSTITIONS?
SHOULD HURACAN GATHER HIS ARMY AT THE GATE OF THE TEMPLE MOUND?
THAT WOULD BE WISE, O MY SUPREME LORD.
NEVER!

ARE THE WORDS OF IKTOMI, THE GREATEST TRICKSTER OF ALL, TO BE CONSIDERED TRUSTWORTHY BY THE SUPREME LORD OF XIBALBA?
FEW MILES NORTH-WEST OF CAHOKIA, A LAKOTA MEDICINE MAN BY THE NAME OF EAGLE OF THE SUN LIES DOWN IN A COMPLETE STATE OF TRANCE ON THE GRASSY PRAIRIE, HIS EYES CLOSED...

THE GATE OF THE TEMPLE MOUND!
CAHOKIA: THE TEMPLE MOUND CITY.
LADINO! TELL THE MEN TO PROPERLY CHECK THIS VILLAGE AND ALL ITS SURROUNDINGS.
ME AND EL CAPITAN MUST INITIATE THE RITE.
MAY THE GREAT MISTERY HELPS US! THESE PALE FACES HAVE DRAGGED US TO A CERTAIN DEATH!

IF I DIE HERE TODAY, MY DEAR ITZEL, KNOW THAT I WILL CARRY YOU IN MY HEART FOR ETERNITY!
AND I SHALL DO THE SAME, MY LOVE.
CAPTAIN RUBIO, MAY I HAVE THE "HAND AND EYE CEREMONIAL MACE"?
YES, MI GENERAL.
THANK YOU, CAPTAIN.
IN THE NAME OF THE COVENANT SWORN BETWEEN THEE AND THE RACE OF MEN, I CALL TO THEE!
HURACAN, SUPREME LORD OF XIBALBA, REMEMBER!
HEARKEN AND REMEMBER!
HURACAN, KING OF NIGHT: OPEN THY GATE TO ME! HURACAN, LORD OF THE BATTLE: OPEN THY GATE TO ME!
HURACAN, SWORD FOR THE GIANT DESCENDANTS: OPEN THY GATE TO ME!
HURACAN, CUSTODIAN OF THE SACRED WRITINGS: OPEN THY GATE TO ME!

LOOK, EAGLE OF THE SUN! WE HAVE ARRIVED TOO LATE!
MY VISION WAS CORRECT, THEN!
WHAT YOUR VISION SAID, *GREAT SHAMAN*?
TO BUILD A **SACRED STONE HOOP** NEAR THE TEMPLE MOUND AND SEEK FOR ITS PROTECTION.
AND WHAT ELSE?
WE MUST SEEK A MYSTERIOUS MAN WEARING A **BLUE MOONSTONE** NECKLACE, FOR HE IS THE **CHOSEN ONE**...
MAY THE *GREAT MYSTERY* BE WITH US. THAT IS ALL I HAVE TO SAY.
GATE OF THE TEMPLE MOUND: **OPEN UNTO ME!**
RUUMMBLE
WHOA!
WE NEED TO GET CLOSER, EAGLE OF THE SUN.
YES, BEAR CLAW. BUT AS QUIET AS A MOUSE.

HURACAN, THE HIGHEST OF THE NINE PRIESTS OF THE ANCIENTS, PASSED THROUGH THE REIGN OF XIBALBA **TO RECLAIM THE UPPER WORLD AS HIS RIGHTFUL POSSESSION!**
BOW DOWN TO HIS WILL, SLAVES, **AND HE SHALL GRANT YOU A NEW LIFE!**

KAPOOO
HAHAHAHA
FLOSH
AAAH
THIS IS BAD MEDICINE!
VOOOOO!!!
AAAARRRGGGHHH!!!!
DO NOT BE FOOLS! BOW DOWN TO THE SUPREME LORD OF XIBALBA AND ALL YOUR WISHES SHALL COME TRUE!
YOU PROMISED US IMMENSE RICHES, DON PEDRO. INSTEAD, YOU MADE A PACT WITH EL DIABLO!
ANYONE ELSE WISH TO COMPLAIN?

BOW DOWN, SLAVES!
MY DEAR ITZEL: WHEN I GRAB YOUR HAND, FOLLOW ME!
WE SHALL ALL DO AS THE SUPREME LORD OF XIBALBA COMMANDS!
AND TO PROVE OUR LOYALTY, WE SHALL OFFER HIM THE HEADS OF THESE TWO NATIVES!
IF DON PEDRO WISHES TO PROVE HIS LOYALTY TO HURACAN, HE SHOULD DO SO NOT BY SHEDDING THE BLOOD OF THE DEFENSELESS, BUT BY DELIVERING THE HEADS OF THE FAR MORE DANGEROUS NATIVES WHO ARE ABOUT TO ATTACK US!
WHAT NATIVES, MY SUPREME LORD?
THEM!
SSSWWIIIIH
AAAH
VAMONOS, HOMBRES! LET'S KILL 'EM ALL!
RAAAH

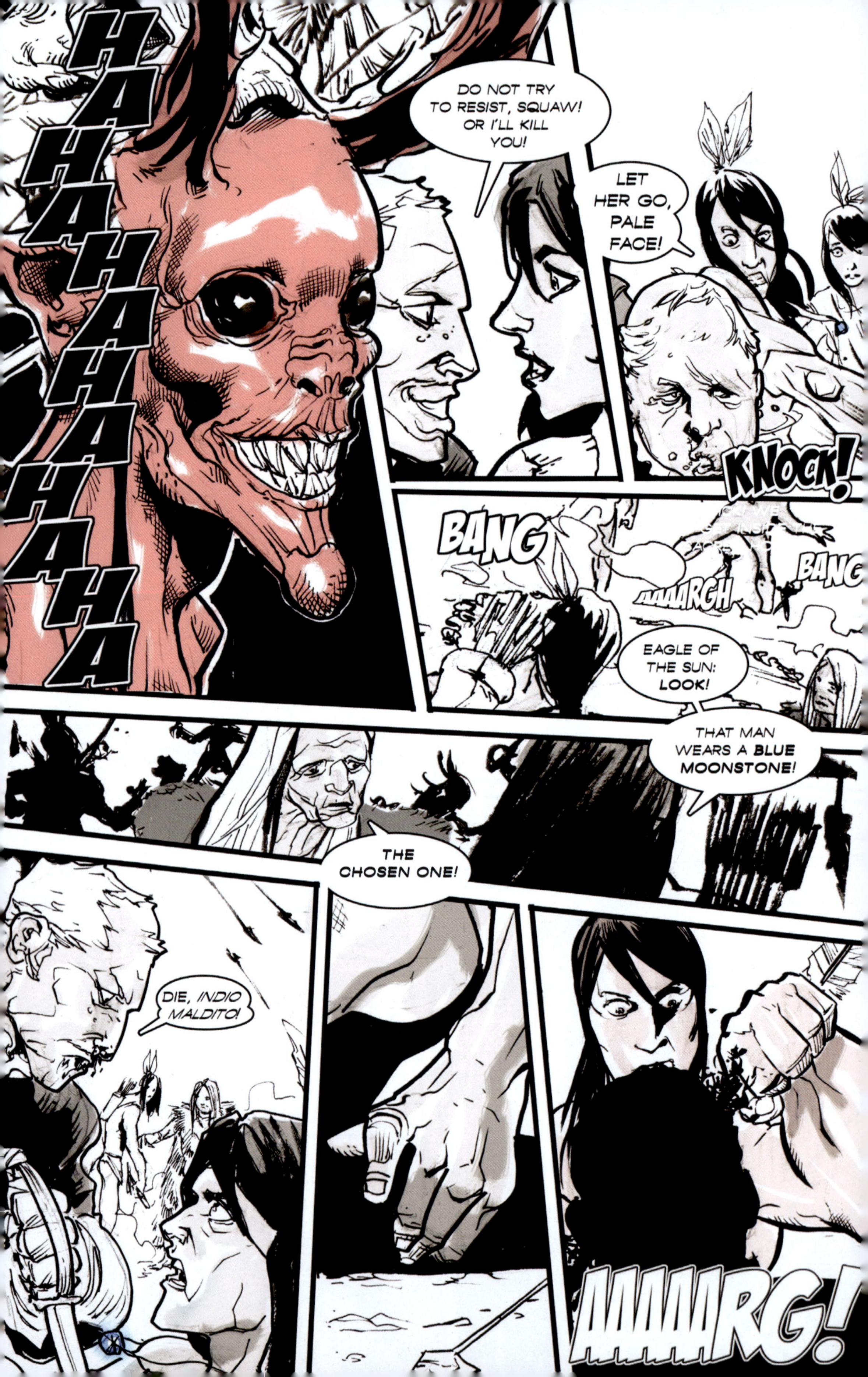
HAHAHAHAHAHAHAHA
DO NOT TRY TO RESIST, SQUAW! OR I'LL KILL YOU!
LET HER GO, PALE FACE!
KNOCK!
BANG
AAAARGH
BANG
EAGLE OF THE SUN: LOOK!
THAT MAN WEARS A BLUE MOONSTONE!
THE CHOSEN ONE!
DIE, INDIO MALDITO!
AAAAARG!

BRING THEM TO MY FEET!
THUMP!
HAHAHA
RUMBLE!
?!
SWIIISH
MY NAME IS TECUMSEH, OF THE CHOCTAW PEOPLE! I HAVE BEEN CHOSEN BY THE MOON GODDESS TO REPULSE YOUR EVIL!
HOW DARE YOU STARE AT THE EYES OF THE SUPREME LORD OF XIBALBA! YOUR HEAD SHALL SOON ADORN MY BELT, SLAVE!

RRRUUMMMBLLLEEEEE
TECUMSEH! YOU'RE ALIVE!
HURACAN'S MEDICINE IS INVINCIBLE AND HIS WILL ETERNAL .
SO HOW COULD THIS BE POSSIBLE?
RRUUUMBLE

AAAAAH
RRRUUMMMBLLLEEEEE
WE MUST JUMP, ITZEL!
I TOLD YOU IKTOMI WAS NOT TO BE TRUSTED!
NOW, LOOK!

IT IS NOT THE TRICKSTER'S FAULT, YOU LURID SIMPLETON!
IT'S THEIRS!
RUMMBLE
AAAAHH
GREAT MANITOU!

NNOOO
WOOOSHHH!!
AAAH
TUMP!

A MYSTERIOUS AND HUMBLE MAN **HAS SAVED MANKIND FROM THE TERRIBLE THREAT OF HURACAN**. WE SHALL RECOUNT HIS BRAVERY TO ALL WHO SHALL LISTEN.
AND LEARN FROM IT!

"LONG AGO, AN OLD LAKOTA SACRED MAN HAD A VISION. IN HIS VISION, IKTOMI, THE GREAT TRICKSTER AND TEACHER OF WISDOM, APPEARED IN THE FORM OF A SPIDER..."
"IKTOMI THE SPIDER PICKED UP THE ELDER'S WILLOW HOOP, WHICH HAD FEATHERS, HORSEHAIR, BEADS AND OFFERINGS ON IT, AND BEGAN TO SPIN A WEB..."
"HE SPOKE TO THE ELDER ABOUT THE CYCLES OF LIFE, HOW WE BEGIN OUR LIVES AS INFANTS, MOVE ON THROUGH CHILDHOOD AND ONTO ADULTHOOD. FINALLY, WE GET OLD, WHERE WE MUST BE TAKEN CARE OF AS INFANTS, COMPLETING THE CYCLE..."
"BUT, IKTOMI SAID, IN EACH TIME OF LIFE THERE ARE MANY FORCES, SOME GOOD AND SOME BAD. IF YOU LISTEN TO THE GOOD FORCES, THEY WILL STEER YOU IN THE RIGHT DIRECTION..."

"BUT, IF YOU LISTEN TO THE BAD FORCES, THEY WILL STEER YOU IN THE WRONG DIRECTION, AND MAY HURT YOU, AS IS IN THEIR NATURE..."

"WHILE THE SPIDER SPOKE, HE CONTINUED TO WEAVE HIS WEB. WHEN IKTOMI FINISHED SPEAKING, HE GAVE THE ELDER THE WEB AND SAID: "THE WEB IS A PERFECT CIRCLE WITH A HOLE IN THE CENTER. USE THE WEB TO HELP YOUR PEOPLE REACH THEIR GOALS, MAKE GOOD USE OF THEIR IDEAS, DREAMS AND VISIONS. IF YOU BELIEVE IN THE GREAT SPIRIT, THE WEB WILL CATCH YOUR GOOD IDEAS AND THE BAD ONES WILL FALL THROUGH THE HOLE..."
IKTOMI

YOU FOLKS ARE PACKIN' GOLD, AIN'T YA, AARON?
TELL THE OTHERS TO KEEP A SHARP EYE OUT . I'LL BE BACK DIRECTLY .

OH, JACK .
IT'S YOU .
ALLIE, WHAT ARE YOU DOING HERE?
I WAS FETCHING SOME WATER .
I GOT A SURPRISE FOR YA.
SPIDERWORTS .
YOUR FAVORITES .
I'M FRIGHTENED, JACK .
NO NEED TO START AN ARGUMENT IN AN EMPTY HOUSE, ALLIE .
I'M PAID TO PROTECT Y'ALL . AND I SHALL DO SO .
YOU DON'T UNDERSTAND, JACK . IT'S THIS VAST TERRITORY . THIS ENDLESS SEA OF PRAIRIE . THIS PUZZLING SILENCE .
THAT'S WHAT FRIGHTENS ME .

I ALWAYS THOUGHT THAT A GIRL SUCH AS YOURSELF WOULD'VE FOUND THIS MAGNIFICENT LANDSCAPE SOMEHOW ROMANTIC .
I RECKON I WAS WRONG .
A.M
NO NEED TO BE SCARED, ALLIE . WE'LL REACH FORT LARAMIE THE DAY AFTER TOMORROW . AND THEN, VIRGINIA CITY
IS ONLY A WEEK'S JOURNEY .
HAVE YOU THOUGHT ABOUT COMING THERE WITH US?
WITH ME?
I'M STILL ... BROKEN, ALLIE . I JUST ROAM THE FRONTIER AND PICK UP THE PIECES . BEEN 4 YEARS NOW .
BUT I RECKON I MIGHT PUT DOWN ROOTS FOR GOOD .
SOMEDAY .
YOUR FATHER .
AM I CORRECT?
HE USED TO TELL ME TO KEEP SKUNKS, LAWYERS AND BANKERS AT A DISTANCE. BUT I RECKON **HE FORGOT TO ADD HIMSELF TO THE LIST**. HE LEFT ALL HIS SINS WITH US. EVENTUALLY, THE REALITY OF THE SITUATION SET IN: MY FATHER WAS JUST... **DIGGIN' HIS OWN GRAVE**. HE TURNED MY BELOVED UNCLE **BELVEDERE** OUT OF THE HOUSE, GUILTY ONLY OF FALLIN' IN LOVE WITH THE WRONG WOMAN. ME? I JUST LEFT ON MY OWN ACCOUNT.
THERE COULD BE A NEW LIFE WAITING FOR YOU AND ME IN MONTANA, JACK . PERHAPS THE TIME HAS COME FOR YOU TO LET GO OF THE PAST .
SOME PEOPLE, LIKE YOUR FATHER, GRIN AND BEAR IT . OTHERS, LIKE YOU, SMILE AND CHANGE IT . ME? **I'M BETWEEN THE DEVIL AND THE DEEP BLUE SEA .**

RRUMMBLE
!
?
SLY AND DANIEL ! THEY'RE BUSHWACKIN' US .
LET'S JOIN THE OTHERS . NOW!

JUST LIKE WE THOUGHT, DANIEL .
WE CAUGHT THESE COCKSUCKERS WITH THEIR PANTS DOWN AND NOW THEY'RE SHAKIN' LIKE A HOUND PISSIN' PEACH PITS .

GITTY-UP, BOYS .
LET'S GIT 'EM ALL CHEWED UP!
BLAM
BANG
STAY HERE.
BANG
AAAAAAH
BANG
BLAM
JACK! DON'T!
I HAVE TO. YOU'LL BE SAFE HERE .
JUST STAY DOWN .
JACK!

BANG
BLAM
BANG
BLAM
I AIN'T INTERESTED IN THE WHOLE KIT AND CABOODLE, CLEM.
JUST THE GOLD. WHERE DID YOU HIDE IT?
ONLY A BUZZARD FEEDS ON HIS FRIENDS.
WE AIN'T FRIENDS. JUST PASSIN' ACQUAINTANCES.

BLAM
AAAAAH
MARY!
NOOOOO!
BLAM

CLACK
CLACK
OOPS ...
CLIC

BLAM!!
I'M GONNA KILL YOUR PRETTY LIL' DAUGHTER TOO IF YOU DON'T TELL ME WHAT I WANNA KNOW.
COMPRENDE?
YOU... BASTARD .
SEEMS LIKE YOU'RE HEADIN' THERE FIRST .
YOU GO TO HELL!
HOLD IT, SLY!

BLAM
YOU SON OF A BITCH!
CLIC
BLAM!

BANG!
ZATT
DAD!
JACK!
NOOOOO!
HERE SHE COMES.
LIKE A DOVE FLYIN' OVER THE EAGLE'S NEST.

BLAM
BLAM BLAM
AAG
AAAAH
BANG
BANG

QUIT THRASHIN' 'BOUT, YOU DAMN FLOOZY!
LEMME GO.

SCRATCH
BOTH YOUR PARENTS AND YOUR BEAU ARE ALREADY WEARIN' A MARBLE HAT. CARE TO JOIN 'EM?
SLAP
BLAM

YOU STUPID BITCH.
BANG

AAAH!
GGGHHH...
<<THESE WASICHU ARE FOOLS !>>*
*TRANSLATED FROM LAKOTA .

JACK ...
JACK ...
I'M... GLAD ... HE IS CHOOSING ... **YOU!**
WHAT?

IKTOMI !
BANG BANG
BLAM BLAM
BLAM
BANG

SLY HEARS THE STRIDES OF SOMETHING APPROACHING. LOOKS UP. IKTOMI STOPS RIGHT IN FRONT OF HIM. THE BANDIT CANNOT BELIEVE HIS EYES...
SSSSSSHHFF

<<IKTOMI THANKS HIS WHITE SLAVE FOR ALLOWING HIM TO RISE AGAIN.>>
SLY! WATCH OUT FOR THAT INJUN!
CHIC

BLAM!
ZZIT
RROOOAR
IIIIH!

<< FEED ME WITH YOUR FEAR, WASICHU . I 'M HUNGRY. >>
<< TRANSLATED FROM LAKOTA >>
ROOOAR
AAAAHH
WHAT THE HELL ...?

JESUS H. CHRIST!
DID YOU SEE THAT?
HE HE HE
BLAM
LET'S KILL THIS SON OF A BITCH!
MEANWHILE, **AARON** MANAGES TO SNEAK AWAY FROM THE MASSACRE...
FRANTIC, HE GETS ON A HORSE, **THREE SACKS OF GOLD** IN ONE HAND, **HERNY RIFLE** IN THE OTHER...
RAAH!
RRAAAASH
HE GALLOPS AWAY, FAST LIKE THE WIND, LEAVING HIS FAMILY AND COMPANIONS TO THEIR OWN DEVICES...

...CRRSSH...
AAH
AAH
BLAM
SATAN HAS COME FOR US!
DANIEL! HOP ON. QUICK!
GASP!

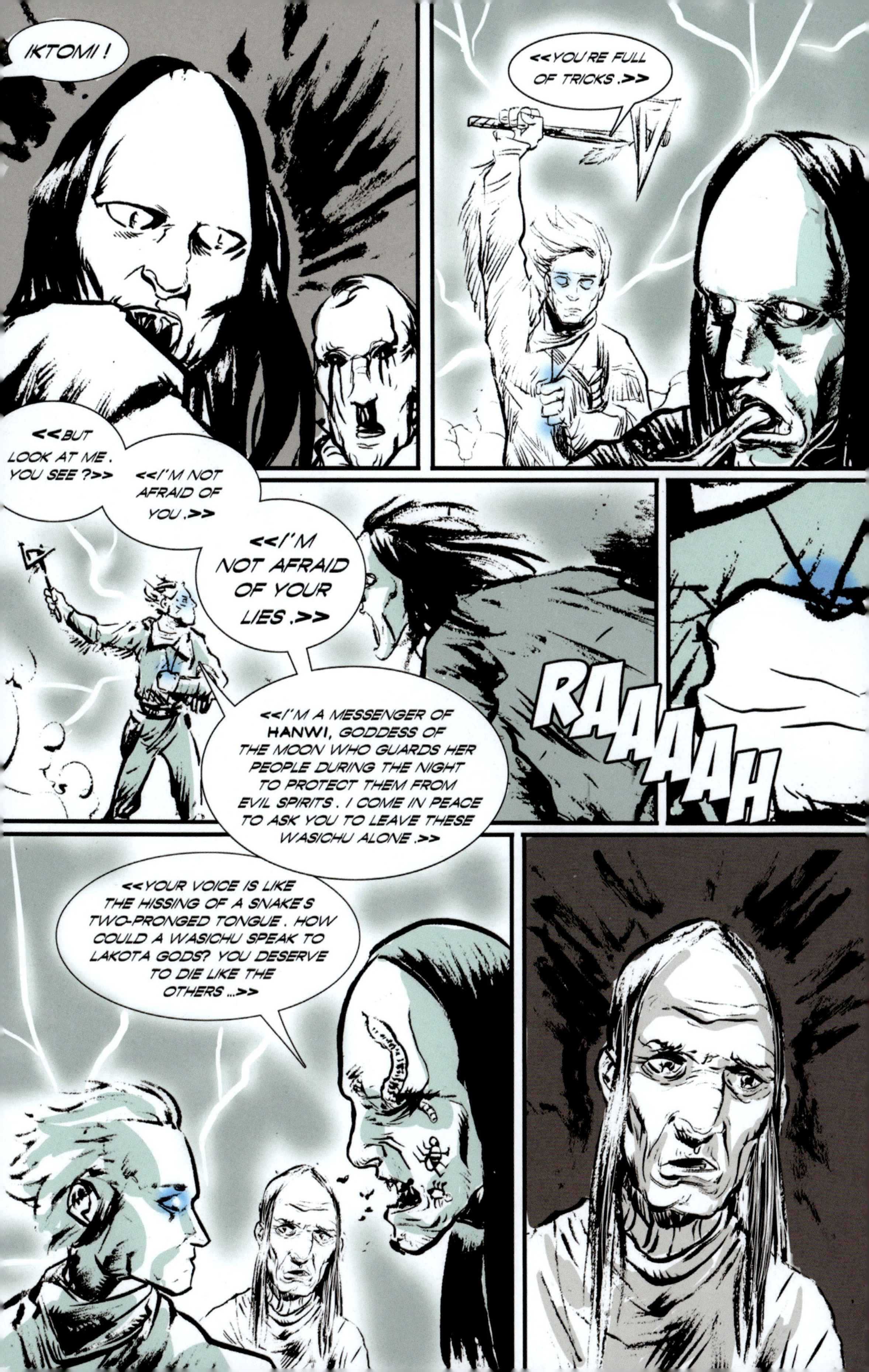
IKTOMI !
<<YOU'RE FULL OF TRICKS.>>
<<BUT LOOK AT ME. YOU SEE?>>
<<I'M NOT AFRAID OF YOU.>>
<<I'M NOT AFRAID OF YOUR LIES.>>
<<I'M A MESSENGER OF HANWI, GODDESS OF THE MOON WHO GUARDS HER PEOPLE DURING THE NIGHT TO PROTECT THEM FROM EVIL SPIRITS. I COME IN PEACE TO ASK YOU TO LEAVE THESE WASICHU ALONE.>>
RAAAAAH
<<YOUR VOICE IS LIKE THE HISSING OF A SNAKE'S TWO-PRONGED TONGUE. HOW COULD A WASICHU SPEAK TO LAKOTA GODS? YOU DESERVE TO DIE LIKE THE OTHERS ...>>

LET'S BURN THE FUCKIN' BREEZE!
<<MAY THE POWER OF THE MOON LIGHT THROW YOU BACK IN THE WATERS OF THE LAKE OF THE SACRED HOOP.>>
RRAAAAH!
THE SHADOW OF IKTOMI GETS SUCKED IN BY THE VORTEX. IN A FEW SECONDS, IKTOMI DISAPPEARS, VANISHING INTO THE SAME WATERS HE CAME FROM...
<<MEDICINE EAGLE IS BEHOLDEN TO THE GREAT HANWI FOR HER HELP AND GUIDANCE.>>

LAKOTA VILLAGE.

<<MY HEART GIVES ME NO REASON TO CALL YOUR STORY INTO QUESTION.
THE WORDS SPOKEN BY A SHAMAN ARE ALWAYS WORDS OF WISDOM. BUT MY MIND WONDERS AND FALLS INTO DOUBT: WHY DID YOU BRING A WOUNDED WASICHU INTO OUR VILLAGE?>>
<<BLUE HORSE CAN MAKE THE WHITE WORDS. HE HOLDS THE ANSWER TO OUR QUESTIONS.>>
<<I THOUGHT YOU SAID THIS WASICHU SPOKE TO IKTOMI IN LAKOTA.>>
<<CERTAIN THINGS CATCH YOUR EYE, BUT PURSUE ONLY THOSE THAT CAPTURE YOUR HEART.>>

<<YOU TRADED BUFFALO HIDES WITH THE WASICHU AT THE FORT. CAN YOU MAKE THE WHITE WORDS ?>>
<<YES .>>
<<OUR THOUGHTS ARE CLOUDED BECAUSE THE SPIRITS ARE RESTLESS. SO I ASK YOU TO SPEAK TO THIS WASICHU. NOT FOR ME, BUT FOR THE WHOLE TRIBE .>>
<<IF THE COUNCIL HAS DECIDED THAT, I WILL NOT TAKE POSITION AGAINST IT. AS AN AKICITA*, IT IS A GREAT HONOR TO BE ABLE TO HELP OUR PEOPLE .>>
*SORT OF "INDIAN POLICE".
WHERE... THE HELL... AM I ?

WHAT HAPPENED TO ME?
WE LAKOTAS. OGLALA. THIS IS VILLAGE OF GREAT CHIEF **SPOTTED ELK** .
YOU SAFE HERE .
MY GIRL . ALLIE . CLEM'S DAUGHTER . **DID SHE MAKE IT?**
ALLIE ...
<<HE'S TALKING ABOUT A WOMAN.>>

<<ASK THE WASICHU IF HE CAN MAKE THE LAKOTA WORDS.>>
THE GREAT SHAMAN ASK IF YOU CAN MAKE THE LAKOTA WORDS.
MY NAME'S JACK FREEMAN. I WAS BORN IN TENNESSEE. MY FATHER OWNED A PLANTATION. WHAT DO YOU THINK?
I DO NOT UNDERSTAND.
NO. I CANNOT. NOT A SINGLE WORD.
<<ASK HIM IF HE RECALLS IKTOMI.>>
IK-WHO? ALL I REMEMBER IS SLY SHOOTIN' AT ME. WHATEVER HAPPENED AFTER THAT IS A BLUR.
<< THIS WASICHU IS A WISACA WAKAN! >>
WOULD SOMEONE BE KIND ENOUGH TO EXPLAIN TO ME WHAT THE HELL IS GOIN' ON HERE?

AAARRGGHH!!!
I GOTTA GET ON THAT HORSE...

ARE YOU...HERE... TO TEND...TO ME, MISS?
NOT QUITE, *WASICHU.* I NEED WHAT'S LEFT OF YOUR LIFE!
NOOOOOOOO!!!
NOOOO!!! PLEASE!!!!
AAAAAHHHH!!!

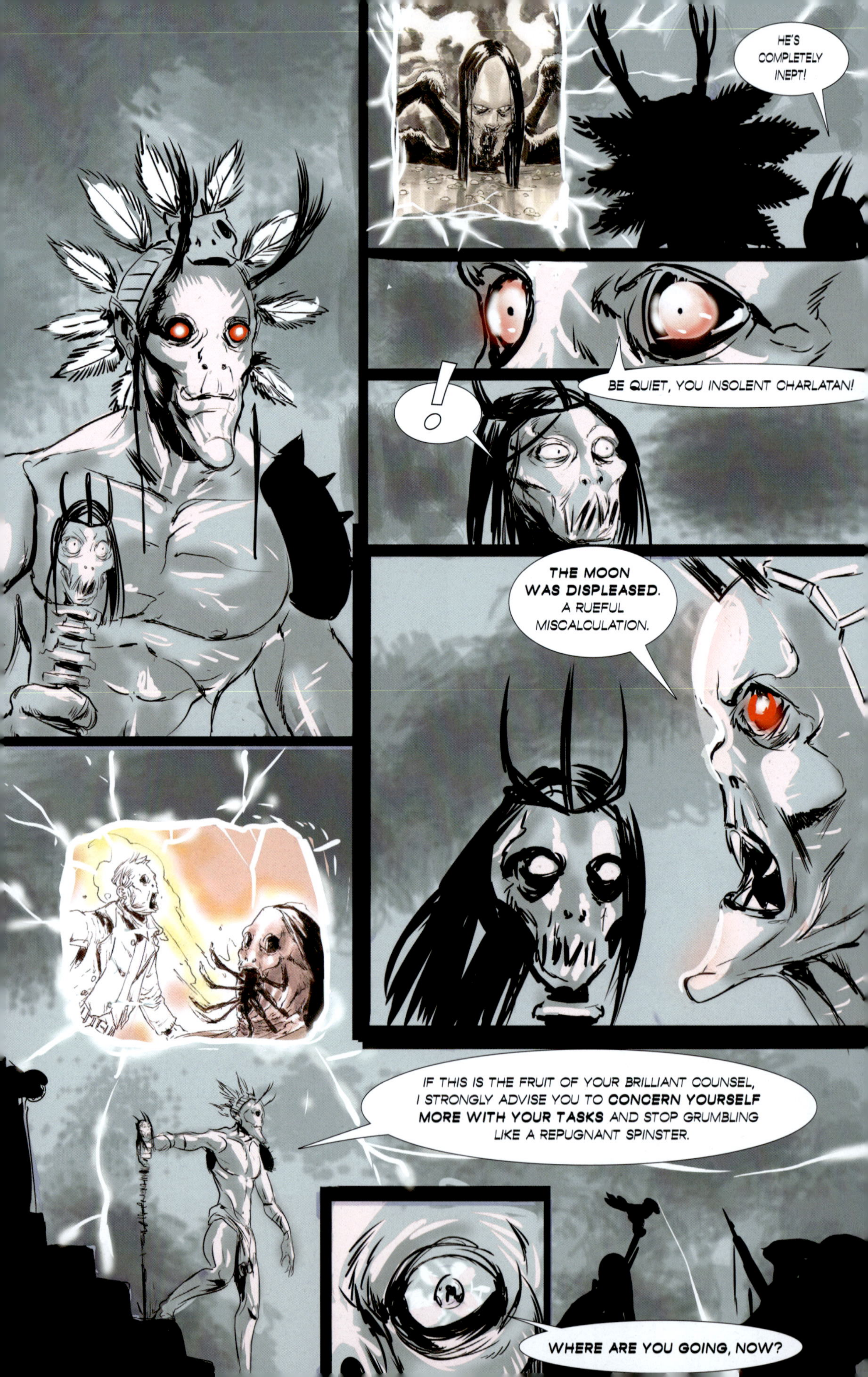
HE'S COMPLETELY INEPT!
BE QUIET, YOU INSOLENT CHARLATAN!
!
THE MOON WAS DISPLEASED. A RUEFUL MISCALCULATION.
IF THIS IS THE FRUIT OF YOUR BRILLIANT COUNSEL, I STRONGLY ADVISE YOU TO CONCERN YOURSELF MORE WITH YOUR TASKS AND STOP GRUMBLING LIKE A REPUGNANT SPINSTER.
WHERE ARE YOU GOING, NOW?

AND ASKING INTRUSIVE QUESTIONS TO YOUR SUPREME LORD, IS **NOT** ONE OF THEM!
YOU'RE WASTING YOUR TIME WITH HER. SHE'S UNDER THE PROTECTION OF THE MOON GODDESS.
NOT FOR LONG!

KRAKATOOM
THOOM

MYRTLE PETTIBONE, VIRGINIA CITY
HENRY BIRD'S NEST
TO MY MIND, WE'VE GOT COMMON INTERESTS. LET'S MAKE A PACT.

IN REGARDS TO WHAT?
THAT FUCKIN' DUST-UP AT THE LAKE, WHAT ELSE? LOOK: I WASN'T BORN IN THE WOODS TO BE SCARED BY AN OWL, BUT I RECKON WE BOTH REALIZED **WHO THAT FUCKIN' DOOHICKEY WAS.**
THE FUCKIN' DEVIL, *COMPRENDE?*
SUPPOSIN' YOU'RE RIGHT: WHAT DO YOU SUGGEST?
TO THROW A VEIL OVER THIS WHOLE FUCKIN' AFFAIR AND NEVER MENTION IT AGAIN.
RUUUMBLEE!
YOU CAN HIDE THE FIRE, **BUT WHAT WILL YOU DO WITH THE SMOKE?**
AIN'T Y'ALL THE OUTRIDERS CONTRACTED BY THEM PROSPECTORS IN **FOREST CITY?**

WHAT'S THAT TO YA, FAT MAN?
AND WHAT THE HELL IS THIS SLOP?
PIONEER CUT DUMPLINGS *, FELLAS. THE ONE AND ONLY HOUSE SPECIALTY. OVERINDULGE YOURSELVES.
* TYPICAL 19TH CENTURY PIONEER FOOD
COCKCHAFERS.

YOUR...FAMILY?
THEY WERE COUNTIN' ON THAT.
A.M.

SOONER OR LATER, SOMEWHERE, SOMEHOW, THESE SONS OF BITCHES WILL SETTLE WITH THE WORLD AND MAKE PAYMENT FOR WHAT THEY HAVE TAKEN.
I SWEAR.

WHAT ARE Y'ALL DOIN'?
GREAT SHAMAN SAY WE MUST BURN BODIES.
WELL, YOU AIN'T GONNA BURN THIS ONE.
WHAT IS THE OLD MAN DOIN'?
BURN CEDAR LEAVES TO PURIFY LAKE.
YOU DON'T LIKE WHITE PEOPLE MUCH, DO YA?
GREAT SHAMAN SAY YOU STRANGE MAN. SAY YOUR BLUE MOONSTONE HAS GREAT POWERS. TIME WILL TELL IF YOU SPEAK WITH STRAIGHT TONGUE.
I MUST APOLOGIZE. I SWUNG MY LEGS FROM A DIME: I FAILED TO KEEP A PROMISE. THIS POOR FOLK'S PLANS HAVE COME A CROPPER IN SUCH A VICIOUS MANNER. AND THE WOMAN I WAS FOND OF HAS PASSED ON. MURDERED BY A HERD OF COWARDS. I'M THIRSTY FOR REVENGE, AND THAT MAKES ME FEEL KINDA...

NONETHELESS, I DON'T RECALL THANKIN' Y'ALL FOR ANYTHING. I DIDN'T EVEN ASK WHAT YOUR NAMES ARE.
NAMES?
ME **BLUE HORSE**. GREAT SHAMAN IS **MEDICINE EAGLE**.
I HEARD YOUR STORY, MEDICINE EAGLE. AND TO BE HONEST WITH YA, YESTERDAY MY LOGIC WOULD'VE CLASSIFIED IT AS A LOAD OF CRAP. BUT, TODAY...
TELL ME: **WHO AM I? WHAT'S HAPPENIN' TO ME?**
<< YOUR HEART HAS BEEN BROKEN, *WASICHU*. NOT JUST TODAY. **BUT MANY WINTERS AGO.** AND IT STILL WANDERS. BUT A PERSON NEEDS TO LOSE HIMSELF IN ORDER TO FIND HIMSELF AGAIN. I'M NOT SAYING THAT YOU SHOULD BURY THE HATCHET. YOU HAVE THE RIGHT TO AVENGE THE DEATH OF YOUR LOVE ONES. BUT IF YOU WANT TO FIND YOUR TRUE SELF, YOU MUST BURY THE PAST. **THERE COULD BE A NEW LIFE WAITING FOR YOU.** >>
THAT'S WHAT ALLIE SAID, WORD FOR WORD. HOW COULD HE POSSIBLY KNOW ALL THIS?
<< *WAKAN TANKA* IS ABOVE EVERYTHING AND GOVERNS EVERYTHING. WHEN *WAKAN TANKA* WISHES ONE OF MANKIND TO DO SOMETHING, **HE MAKES HIS WISHES KNOWN.** EVERYTHING ON THE EARTH HAS A PURPOSE. EVERY DISEASE AN HERB TO CURE IT. AND EVERY PERSON A MISSION. *HANWI*, OUR MOON GODDESS, HAS SHOWED ME YOURS: **TO LEARN THE SACRED MAN WAY.** >>
<< YOU CAN GET ON THAT HORSE AND RIDE AWAY. WE WILL NOT STOP YOU. **NO MAN CAN TELL ANOTHER MAN WHAT TO DO.** >>
<< BUT IF **TWO MOON** DECIDES TO STAY, **I SHALL TEACH HIM THE SHAMAN WAY.** >>

WHO'S **TWO MOON?**
MEDICINE EAGLE WISH TO TEACH TWO MOON HOW TO BECOME A SHAMAN.
THAT IS THE NAME GREAT SHAMAN HAS CHOSEN FOR YOU.
<< TO BLUE HORSE I SAY: DO NOT JUDGE YOUR NEIGHBOR UNTIL YOU HAVE WALKED TWO MOONS IN HIS MOCCASINS. TO THE *WASICHU* I SAY: I SHALL TEACH HIM HOW TO BE MASTER OF HIMSELF SO THAT HE CAN GET HIS REVENGE. SHARING AND GIVING ARE THE WAY OF THE *GREAT MYSTERY*. I AM NOT HERE ONLY TO POINT OUT THE WAY, BUT TO LEAD THE WAY. **WILL TWO MOON FOLLOW IT? >>**
?!
!
END OF VOLUME ONE...

TO BE
CONTINUED...